And they **love** all of the same things: **splashing** in the lake,

eating **big juicy** worm burgers,

making **massive** mud men and . . .

playing in a

Ig
and
Og!

super cool,

crazy loud,

totally
rocking,

ROCK BAND!

One morning, Ig went off
to meet Og at the lake.

But Og was
NOT
alone.

He was floating along
with **someone else**

and they looked like they were the **best** of friends.

"Hi, I'm Bog Frog!" she said. "Bog for short."

Ig thought she was very small, very yellow, and very slimy.

Ig was **NOT** happy. And he did **NOT** like floating.

Ig liked . . .

"Bog is ruining everything," Ig muttered.
Ig was NOT happy.

And his tummy was rumbling.
He was looking forward to his worm burger for lunch, but . . .

Bog took them to her favourite restaurant.

Ig didn't like the food.

And the food didn't like Ig either!

"Bog is ruining everything!" wailed Ig.

Ig **was NOT** happy.

After lunch it was time for band practice.

But Bog was
so super cool,

and
crazy
loud,

and
totally
rocking,

that Og didn't even notice Ig's amazing drumming!
He only had eyes for Bog.

Ig was NOT happy.
HE HAD HAD ENOUGH!

Now nobody was happy,

and everything was broken.

Ig was all alone.

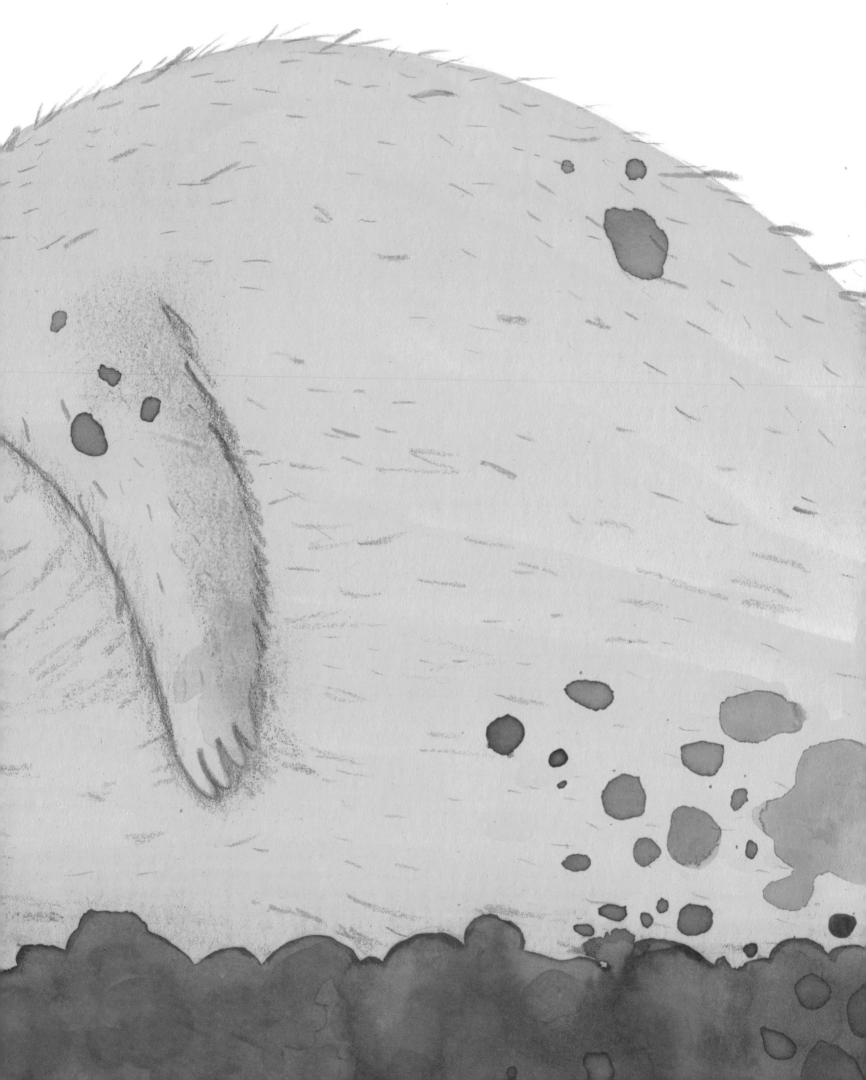

He tried to pretend that
Og was still there.

HA HA

Then he was angry that
Og wasn't there.

Og and Bog were together. Just the two of them.

It **was NOT** fair!

So he marched off to find them,
feeling cross. But when
he got there . . .

Bog was fixing Ig's drum kit and Og was preparing a worm burger picnic to say sorry.

Ig was still not happy
and he was going to tell them.
But his tummy was rumbling.

So first . . .

... he thought he might have
a little taste of a
worm burger.

And then he tried
a small slurp
of lemonade.

To finish, he scoffed a slice
of cake. It was delicious!

Soon, he was having so much
fun, that he forgot all about
being cross.

He was starting to feel different.
He was starting to feel happy.
REALLY happy!

Maybe having Bog around wasn't so bad after all.
Maybe having **two** best friends was **better**
than having one!

"I'm sorry," said Ig, hugging both his friends. "I was **super jealous, crazy mean** and **totally grumpy!**"

"We're so sorry too, Ig," said Og.

"And **we** didn't mean to leave you out," said Bog.

And then Ig felt so happy
that he started **tapping**.

Then Og started **strumming**,
and so Bog started **humming**.

So Ig started **drumming**,
then Og started **rocking** and . . .

Bog started SINGING!

Ig, Og and Bog played and played and played,
and they were so **super cool**,
crazy loud and
totally rocking . . .

... that soon **everyone** wanted to join the band!

Audition to play with Ig, Og + Bog TODAY! ARE YOU SUPER COOL CRAZY=LOUD= AND TOTALLY ROCKING?

IG PIG AND OG FROG is a DAVID FICKLING BOOK
First published in Great Britain in 2020 by David Fickling Books,
31 Beaumont Street, Oxford, OX1 2NP 978-1-78845-089-8 www.davidficklingbooks.com
This edition published 2021
Text and illustration © Sophie Burrows, 2020   1 3 5 7 9 10 8 6 4 2
The right of Sophie Burrows to be identified as the author and illustrator of this work has been asserted in accordance with the Copyright,
Designs and Patents Act 1988. No part of this publication may be reproduced, stored in a retrieval system, or transmitted in any form
or by any means, electronic, mechanical, photocopying, recording or otherwise, without the prior permission of the publishers.

MIX
Paper from
responsible sources
FSC® C104723

All rights reserved. WARNING: This book is TOTALLY ROCKING!
Papers used by David Fickling Books are from well-managed forests and other responsible sources.
DAVID FICKLING BOOKS Reg. No. 8340307 A CIP catalogue record for this book is available from the British Library.
Printed and bound in China by Toppan Leefung. Edited by Alice Corrie & designed by Ness Wood